W9-AHM-621

NOVEMBER

Thanksgiving is celebrated on the fourth
Thursday of November.

Thanksgiving reminds people of the Pilgrims many years ago. The Pilgrims wanted to worship God in their own way, which they had not been allowed to do.

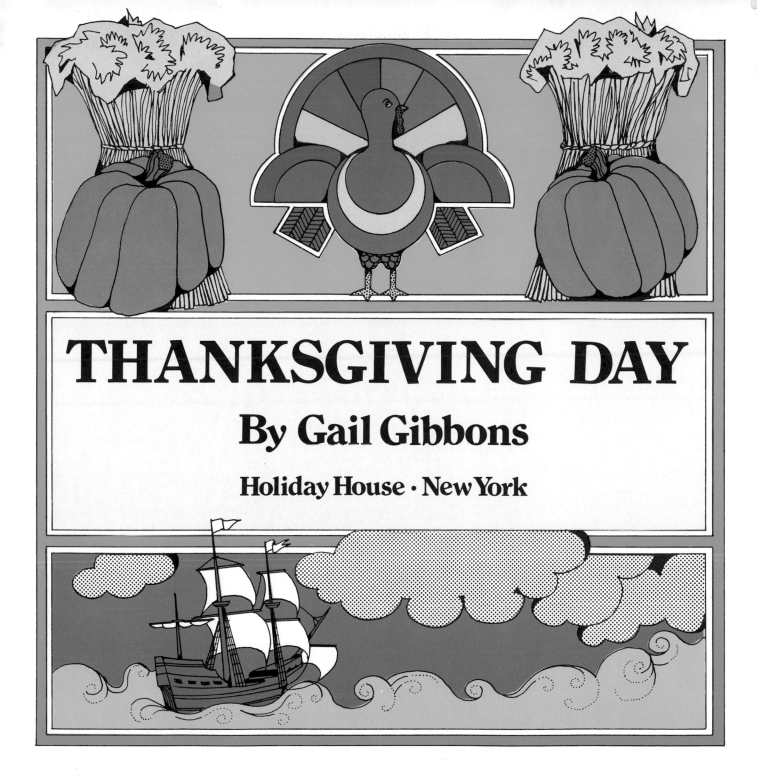

THANKSGIVING DAY

By Gail Gibbons

Holiday House · New York

For MICHAEL COOPER

Copyright © 1983 by Gail Gibbons
All rights reserved
Printed in the United States of America

Library of Congress Cataloging in Publication Data

Gibbons, Gail.
Thanksgiving Day.

Summary: Presents information about the first
Thanksgiving and the way that holiday is celebrated
today.
1. Thanksgiving Day—Juvenile literature. [1.
Thanksgiving Day]   I. Title.
GT4975.G53   1983   394.2′683   83-175
ISBN 0-8234-0489-7
ISBN 0-8234-0576-1 (pbk.)

They left their homes in England and sailed across the ocean to the New World in a ship called the Mayflower.

The voyage was difficult and stormy. The Mayflower was
very crowded, too. Many of the Pilgrims became sick.

Finally, after many weeks, they sighted land. They rowed
to the shores of America to begin their new lives.

They began building homes.

The cold winter came. The Pilgrims had little food to eat, and some of them died.

Spring finally arrived. Friendly Indians showed the
Pilgrims how to plant corn, beans, and pumpkins.

The Pilgrims learned how to hunt better, too.

Their crops grew and grew. When fall came their harvest was great. The Pilgrims wanted to thank God for the food they would have through the cold winter months.

They decided to have a Thanksgiving feast. The Pilgrims invited their Indian friends.

They had wonderful food to eat. There was turkey with nuts, herbs, bread, and cranberries. They made sauce from the cranberries.

They roasted deer meat. There was cornbread, beans, and pumpkin pie.

The Pilgrims and Indians played many games and shared happy times together.

The feast lasted three days. There was much to be thankful for.

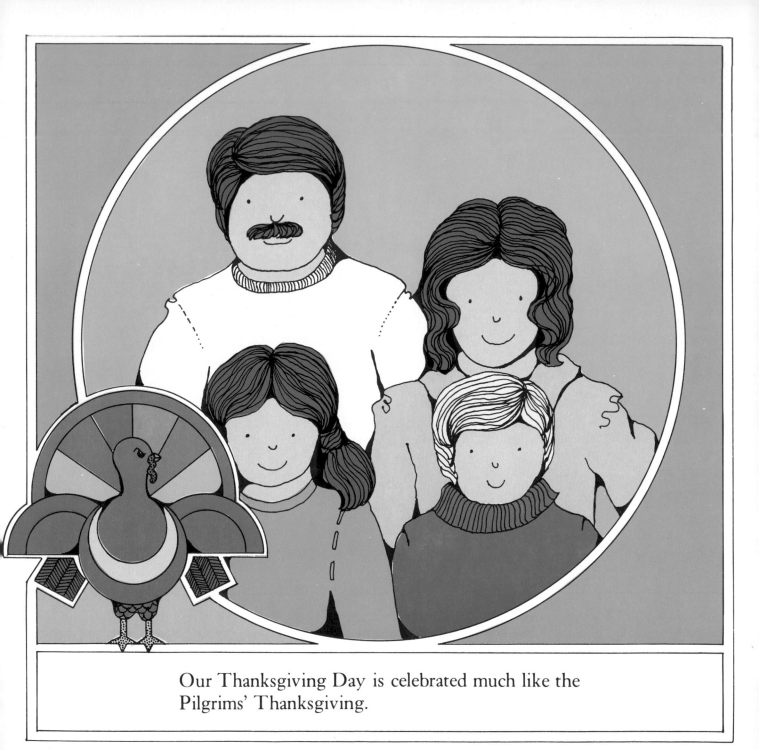

Our Thanksgiving Day is celebrated much like the Pilgrims' Thanksgiving.

Some homes are decorated. Cornstalks are gathered together and arranged with pumpkins, gourds, and colorful fall leaves to look like harvest time.

Pictures of the Pilgrims and turkeys appear in windows and on doors.

Sometimes candles are lit.

Horns of plenty, representing a bountiful harvest,
may also be used for decoration.

Hymns of Thanksgiving are sung, and prayers and blessings are spoken.

Families and friends gather together for a feast.

Many tables are filled with the same foods the Pilgrims and Indians shared.

There is cranberry sauce and a big turkey stuffed with
bread crumbs, herbs, and nuts.

Also there are sweet potatoes, beans, squash, and cornbread.

Sometimes there is a tasty pumpkin pie for dessert.

Games are played.

There are grand parades to watch.

People ride on floats and there is music.

On Thanksgiving Day there is much to be thankful for.